About the Author

James Tonks lives near the village of Stibb in North Cornwall. He is a primary school teacher, and spends his spare time surfing, writing and walking in Stowe woods.

THE SWORD WATCHERS

JAMES TONKS

ILLUSTRATIONS BY LOUISE BØHLING

PINNACLE HOUSE

A Catalogue record for this book is available from the British
Library.

ISBN 0 9541242 0 0

Typeset and Graphic Design
by Katie Cobbledick, Bude, Cornwall,EX23 9PU

Printed and bound in Great Britain
by Ebenezer Baylis & Son Ltd, The Trinity Press,
London Rd, Worcester, WR5 2JH

Pinnacle House,
4 Cheswick Way, Solihull, West Midlands, B90 4EX.

This book is dedicated to the memory of

Richard Ensor
(Feb 1988-Aug 2001)

"A most brave and noble dragon"

Chapter One

The Secret Legend Of Stowe Woods.

The mist lingered over the black waters of the lake in the dank cold air, on a late October afternoon long ago. Through the trees of the woods that surrounded the lake came the terrible sounds of battle; the distant cries of dying men and the clashing of metal.

The echo of branches cracking could be heard somewhere close to the shores of the lake, as a boy of eleven forced his way through the undergrowth. His heart pounded so strongly that it felt as if it might burst through his chest. He raced along, not caring for the scratches from the thorny bushes, or his bruised cut legs. For not far behind him came the baying of hounds and the shouts of his pursuers.

"He's down near the lake edge sire!" came a breathless voice from above him.

A deeper and angrier voice sounded back. "He must not reach the lake!"

But it was too late, for now the boy stood at the bottom of the bank near to the water. In his hand he clutched a golden sword by its handle, and he raised it above his head, about to fling it into the lake.

At the top of the bank appeared a figure cloaked in black sitting on a horse. A hood concealed his face with its dark shadow. His eyes were barely visible, and appeared as two pale slits through the darkness within. The boy was frozen with fear at the sight of the figure, and for a few brief seconds, neither the boy nor the figure moved or made a sound as they faced each other.

Then angrily the figure demanded, "You are beaten! Now give the sword to me so that I may spare you."

The boy thought back to the battlefield. He was just a homeless beggar that the king, Arthur, had taken in, to work as a stable boy for his horses. He had followed Arthur and his knights secretly, and at the moment that he saw Arthur struck down, he had raced across the open ground to where the dying king lay.

"To the lake my boy, run to the lake and throw the sword in so that man shall be safe from all that its magic could release. You are the future. If you fail in this, then all will be lost."

Now the boy looked to the ground, then slowly his eyes lifted up the bank to the menacing figure. He was scared, but he felt his courage rising within him.

"I would rather die than give it to you!" came the

boy's cornered reply. With that he turned and hurled the sword across the open water with all his strength. Behind him rose a cry of anguish from the figure, as a maiden's hand broke the surface of the lake and caught the sword by its handle. A jewel at the centre gave a brilliant sparkle, and the hand and sword disappeared down into the lake once more.

But now the boy was alone and the figure's attention was fixed firmly upon him. He drew his own black sword from his side and held it above him with his arm outstretched. Then he pointed it at the boy. His voice was unnaturally soft, "You are as foolish as you are weak!" Then he raised his voice in anger once more, "Now, if death is your choice then so be it!" And he launched his horse into a full charge through the trees and down the bank towards the boy.

The boy turned and plunged into the cold water with a loud splash, and with that, he was gone.

The figure sat, sword still raised, on his horse as it paced the bank with its nostrils flaring. He scanned the water for signs of life, but only a bubble rose from the depth beneath.

His servant, who had been watching from under a tree at the top of the bank, crept cautiously through the autumn leaves on the slope, building up the courage to speak. "Sire, no one can hold their breath for this long, he must have drowned."

"Silence you fool!" came the enraged reply, "Search the lake!" With that the figure turned and galloped furiously away through the trees.

In fear of his master's anger, the servant searched the lake for days, but found no trace of the boy.

In the centuries following the battle, the story of the lake became lost in time. Many times a mysterious boy was seen. On one occasion when two children lost their way in the woods, a boy guided them to the safety of the village that stood on the hill-top above the trees. According to the story, at his side hung a golden sword of such beauty and brilliance, that it hurt the children's eyes to look upon it. With the passing of the years this story became just another legend.

Chapter Two

The First Day Of The New Term.

It was ten minutes to nine when the bell rang out across the old school yard, in the little stone village of Kilkhampton, in a remote part of North Cornwall. Simon and his sister Rebecca climbed from the seat of their father's old blue Landrover and walked in through the gate.

Simon turned to his Dad. "Where do you think you're going?" he asked.

"Well, I just thought you might like me to come in with you and make sure you're alright. The first day in a new school can be difficult."

"Dad, how old are we?" asked Rebecca grinning.

"Well, Simon here's eleven and that makes you nearly ten Princess," replied her father, half expecting to be told off for calling her Princess.

Rebecca scowled, "If I'm a Princess, then you must be a toad!"

"I suppose I ought to hop off then. Good-bye. Enjoy your first day and don't forget to work hard. Hey

Simon, look after the Princess."

Simon nodded and the two of them walked along the path to the entrance.

Rebecca placed a hand upon the rough grey blocks of the wall outside. "It's different from our school in London. Look how old everything looks. It's more like a church or an old house than a school."

"Do you know there are only sixty-five children here?" said Simon gloomily, "and year five and six are just one class."

Rebecca smiled and placed a hand upon his shoulder. "Just think, we can sit together and everything."

An alarmed expression flashed across Simon's face at the thought of sitting next to his sister, and he gave a sudden snort of nervous laughter. "Oh good," he muttered sarcastically.

They walked through the door and into a large classroom with windows that were too high to see out of. A polished wooden floor caused their footsteps to echo loudly, as they made their way across the room full of children reading silently.

"Ah, you must be Simon and Rebecca, do come in," said the teacher encouragingly, "I'm Miss Jones and this is class three. Well, you're not the only new people to start this year. This is Joe. He tells me he lives in Stibb. Isn't that the village where your father lives?"

"Yes, but we only got here this weekend, so we haven't met anyone yet," answered Rebecca smiling at Joe.

Joe smiled back and nodded at Simon.

Miss Jones' glasses glinted in the light, "Well I think it's good that you all live so close to each other and that you are all new. Stibb has only got about seven houses if I recall. Most of the children here live either out on farms or in the village. Now take a seat at this table here and we can do the register."

For the rest of the morning the children were so busy that they hardly spoke, and it was break time before Simon and Rebecca found themselves together again. Joe, who was even more bewildered than they were, stood close by as an enormous circle of curious children gathered around them on the school playground.

"Where are you from then?" asked a boy from the class.

"London, only our dad is from here," said Simon suspiciously.

"He talks funny," said one of the year six girls.

"Well I think he sounds nice," commented her friend.

Simon turned a little pink. They seemed friendly enough but he was shy and he desperately needed to escape from the attention he was getting.

"That's it, lets play football", he said to the boy in front of him. "Are you coming Joe?"

Joe stood and thought for a second. "Well, if I'm honest I never played it, so I don't think so."

"Don't be so daft, nobody reaches year six without ever playing football," laughed Rebecca, "I only have to stand still and the ball comes to me."

Simon smiled proudly, for in fact Rebecca was without doubt one of the best footballers in her old school.

"Yes of course," said Joe. "What I meant was I haven't played for a while, so please remind me how to play."

Before anyone could stop her, Rebecca babbled out the entire rulebook including tips on kicking a ball properly.

"And that's about it," she gasped.

They moved to the centre of the playground and the younger children moved out of their way.

"Joe, you can take the centre first with Rebecca," said Simon.

"Okay, look Joe," whispered Rebecca in a low voice, "I pass to you, then you get as far as you can, then pass back, and I'll do the rest."

Joe smiled. "If I get to the goal..." he said.

"You won't," interrupted Rebecca "but if you do, then just kick it past the keeper and into the net."

She passed the ball, and she could not believe her eyes when she saw what happened next. Joe moved with the ball. He flicked it over the first boy's head, then spun with it balancing on his toe round the second boy. He pushed it through the third boy's legs and stepped sideways out of Simon's way, who stumbled past him. Then he delivered a kick of such incredible power that it was almost too quick to see, and the ball nearly broke a hole through the net.

The football group fell silent. Simon was first to speak and he was a little cross. "I thought you said you never played football!"

"Well I....." Joe was cut off by the sound of the bell ringing, and the stampede of children racing in to hang up their coats.

By lunch time the incident with the football was forgotten, and the three new ones sat together at a table and chatted happily.

"Well Joe, what do you think of it here?" asked Rebecca chirpily.

"It's nice," he replied with a big grin.

"Is it better than your old school?"

There was a long pause while Joe pondered the

question before he gave a slight nod. "Yes I think so."

"Where do you live anyway?" asked Simon.

"Oh, well it is a little hard to describe," Joe answered cautiously. "It's down in the woods away from the road."

Rebecca frowned. "How can that be? My dad told me that there aren't any houses in the woods!"

Simon rocked back on his chair whilst he thought for a second. His father had been born in Stibb and he knew the area very well. He pulled himself upright again. "Well, perhaps you can come and visit us after school. Then you can take us there."

Joe glanced down nervously. "I can't at the moment. You see, I've lost something and I have to spend some time trying to find it."

Rebecca clapped her hands together. "No problem, we'll help you. What have you lost anyway?"

"I-I can't tell you," said Joe stiffly.

Rebecca stared at Simon, who scornfully shrugged his shoulders as the bell rang for the start of the afternoon.

The end of school was a relief to Rebecca and Simon. They raced out to the old blue Landrover, to see who would get there first and have the front seat. The children's father sat reading the paper as they climbed into the front together.

"How was school?" he asked.

"Fine," they both replied at the same time.

"I see there's an antique show at the church hall in town tonight. We could take that rusty old sword of your grandfather's, the one that hangs over the fireplace. I'd love to know how old it is. Do you know, he got it from his father, and he got it from his father before him and so on? That old sword goes all the way back in history. It could be worth a fortune."

Rebecca giggled, and Simon glared at her. "I'm sorry," she said. "It just seems very unlikely that such a rusty old bit of metal could be worth anything."

As crazy as the idea sounded, Simon liked it. It wasn't as if they had anything else planned for the evening, and this was exactly the sort of thing that made his father unusual. It made quite a change from their mother who worked as a solicitor in London. Their mum and dad had been divorced for five years, and were still friends, but they were so different it was impossible to see why they got married to begin with. "Well we haven't got anything to lose by going along to find out," he said supportively.

"That's it settled then," said their father cheerfully, and the Landrover jerked forwards into the road that led to Bude.

They reached the small town to find that it was busy, and it was difficult to find a parking space near to the church hall. After several chaotic minutes of being pulled around through various crowded rooms, the two children found themselves standing in a queue of people holding all sorts of old objects. The chance of getting someone to look at the sword seemed slim, given the number of people waiting in the line. Simon clutched the sword in his hand, and Rebecca kept tapping the end of it with her foot, which was annoying him. Their father was talking to someone he knew and had his back to them.

Suddenly Simon felt a hand upon his shoulder, and he turned round to see a tall thin woman dressed in a black coat and skirt. Red shoes matched a scarf that hung around her neck, and the overpowering scent of strong perfume lingered upon her.

She was gripping him with considerable strength, and the veins on her hand began to swell underneath her white skin. Her piercing eyes stared into his, and she drew her lips back into a sneer before she leaned forward to speak to him. "I haven't seen you before. Is this your sister? What a pretty thing, and where do you live? I see, is that the place on the hill? And which house would that be? Now give the sword to me."

Simon had not answered any of her questions. He had not said a word, though now he wanted to speak. He opened his mouth, but no sound came out. It was as if the room was still. He was aware of movements, but everything seemed to be in slow motion, and sounds seemed quiet and distant. He felt his feet turn cold, as if some invisible mist were swirling around them. Then he heard the sound of his father's voice saying, "Is my Simon behaving?"

"Oh yes," said the lady, "I was just admiring the sword. Well, must be off, I have an appointment."

With that the lady disappeared into the crowd.

"What a strange one she was," said Simon's dad. "Just think, there you were giving her the sword and talking to her like you knew her. You too Rebecca. I mean, you know better than to talk to strangers anyway, even if she was being friendly."

But Simon made no reply. Instead he just stared down to his hand, which was still holding up the sword for the woman to take. Then he looked at Rebecca, who was staring back at him equally as shocked and amazed at what had just happened. But she could not feel the sword and the mysterious intense warmth that was radiating from its handle.

Chapter Three

A Nightmare Visitor.

The children didn't speak about what had happened until they were back in the Landrover. They drove out of the town and up onto the coastal lane that wound its way through the hills paralleling the cliffs back to Stibb. There were no streetlights out there, and all, except for that which moved within the Landrover headlamps, was totally black.

Inside the cab, both Simon and Rebecca sat on the large front bench seat while they discussed the strange meeting with the woman. Simon also told her about the heat that he had felt coming from the handle of the sword.

Rebecca gave him a disagreeable glance. "Are you sure it wasn't just that you were nervous," she said. "If your hands were sweaty you might have thought that there was heat coming from it, when in fact there wasn't."

"What are you two talking about?" interrupted the children's father. "This sounds like a pretty daft conversation to me."

He was a no nonsense sort of person who laughed

at what he called 'people's overactive imaginations.' Even so, he had secretly found the entire situation a little bit strange.

* * * * * * *

For the next two days the children settled into work at school, and their father was busy decorating their rooms.

It was midnight at the end of the second day, and the children were asleep in their beds, when he experienced a second strange encounter to remind him of the children's conversation.

He was sitting by the fire inside the small lounge at the cottage. It had been a long day and the heat of the room and the dim light made him feel drowsy. It wasn't long before he slipped into sleep. He was disturbed moments later by the sound of the wind rattling the window, but it was a sound he recognised and he roused slowly from his slumber. He turned his head towards the glass, and to his horror, he caught sight of the outline of a person through the darkness outside. The hair on his neck began to stand up, and he felt a cold sweat break out onto his brow. Yet there was no one there. He shook his head and laughed to himself. "Silly me, I'm jumping at my own reflection now."

But then, from the corner of his eye he noticed a flicker at the other window. He turned sharply to face it, the hairs on his neck tingled once again, and his heart thumped loudly sending his blood racing through his veins. There was no mistake this time. He had seen something.

A sudden rush of cold air came down the chimney and into the room, burying the fire in soot so that its flame died. Its chill reached out and caused the man to feel a shudder as the air passed by.

"Unusual wind!" he muttered to himself. But barely had the words escaped his lips when the door began to rattle furiously, as if someone, or something, were hammering upon it from the other side. The children's father stood still. His breathing was shallow and fast, and he felt sick with fear, but he moved slowly towards the door, slid back the latch, and began to turn the brass doorknob.

Having turned it as far as he could, he flung the door open, but at the moment he did, the wind fell still. He stood in the doorway, his rapid breath sending clouds of mist into the damp night air. All was silent. He stepped back in to the room and pushed the lock firmly back into place.

"Like I thought, just the wind," he said to himself. He turned the light off, and hurriedly climbed the cottage stairs to bed.

In the back of his mind he was disturbed by these weird events, as he could not remember a wind so strange, or a night so odd. For most of the night he lay awake wondering about the experience.

Out in the field behind the house, standing in the shadow of the hedge was the tall, thin figure of a woman. She was robed in black, and a sneer revealed her glistening teeth to the night.

She watched the light being turned off downstairs, and now she stood motionless, staring at the cottage.

Upstairs in a small room, Simon lay sleeping soundly. In his dreams he saw a golden sword with a jewel that sparkled at the base of its handle where the blade started. Two silver dragons shone out through the gold on each edge of the blade.

Then the blade was gone, and a dark shadow-like figure sat on a horse looking down upon him. He could not make out the creature's face, but could see two white slits where its eyes should be. Its voice thundered into Simon's sleeping mind.

"Bring the sword to me. Leave your bed and take the sword to the window."

Simon began to stir in his sleep. Slowly, he sat up and placed his feet upon the floor. He moved silently to the door of his bedroom, and then left the room in the direction of the stairs. The boys feet slid gently into place on each step, as he descended the stairs and moved into the lounge, where the rusty old sword hung on the wall above the fireplace.

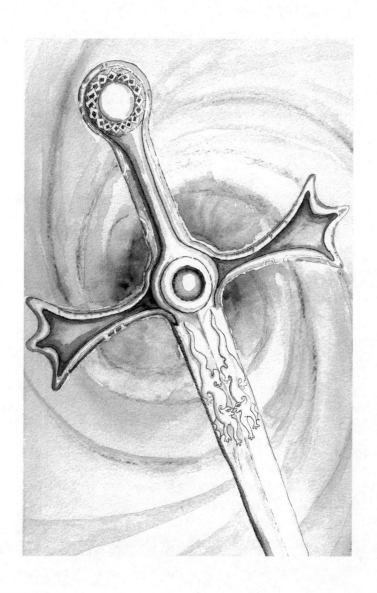

In Simon's mind he was now in the grip of a terrifying nightmare, from which he desperately wanted to wake up. The figure leaned towards him and stretched out a bony hand.

Simon reached for the place where the sword hung but felt only the cold wall. The sword was not there, and he woke with a sudden jolt.

"Looking for this?" came Rebecca's voice from behind him. Simon turned around.

"I don't-don't know what I'm doing," he replied. "I just had a strange dream telling me to get the sword and take it to the window."

Rebecca looked at him thoughtfully. "I had a dream about a beautiful golden sword with a jewel near the handle, and a silver dragon on each blade edge. So I came down to see if it was like our old sword, and look here, you can make out the shape of the dragons, and there's a hole here where there was once a jewel."

Simon was still not completely free of his nightmare, "I was supposed to take the sword to the window."

Rebecca walked over to where he stood, her eyes twinkled with excitement and she whispered, "Simon, that's not all. The handle, it's just like when you met that strange woman. It's warm!"

Simon was awake now and his eyes widened.

"Then that must mean," he paused, "she might be close by; she may even be outside the window!"

They both stood looking into each other's eyes, and then they turned their heads towards the window. The first signs of the new day lightened the sky. The children pushed their faces to the glass and peered out scanning the fields and hedgerows for signs of anyone or anything unusual, but of course, there was nothing there. Whoever had been outside below the window had disappeared in the early dawning light.

* * * * * * *

In the room upstairs the children's father was awake. He heard the floorboards creak, as the children passed over them on their way back to bed, but once again he told himself it must be the wind. He felt a little foolish, that he, a grown man, should have felt so scared. He had lived out in the countryside all his life. He was used to the sounds of his old cottage when the wind blew across the rafters, and yet he couldn't help feeling uncomfortable.

The grey light of dawn poured in through the window. It would soon be time to get the children up for school, so he slipped on his dressing gown and went downstairs to put the kettle on. He passed the sword hanging inconspicuously above the fireplace and went into the kitchen.

He was standing at the sink running over the events of the previous evening, when he noticed deep white marks running across the glass pane in front of him. The marks resembled frost, and yet they were narrow.

He went over to the door and drew back the latch, and then went out and round to the window to examine the marks from the outside. In the early light of the day, small fragments of glass sparkled on the windowsill. He touched the marks. They were deep grooves. Grooves that had cut into the glass, like scratch marks perhaps. He thought for a moment, trying to come up with some kind of explanation for the damage.

He shook his head. "This has been a strange night," he said to himself, and he walked back across to the door, but then he stopped dead in his tracks. His blood turned to ice and the hair on his neck stood up with fear as it had the night before.

The front of the door had great gouges taken out of it. Paint had been scratched off and deep ruts and splinters hung from every groove. He remembered how violently the door had rattled the previous night. Now the intense rattling made sense, for it must have been some kind of animal trying to get in. Yet it made no sense at all. No animal could do such damage.

He remembered how he had bravely flung the door open, and he looked at the deep scratches that had been torn into the tough oak. He felt weak at the knees when he thought of the strength of such an animal that could tear through oak as if it were cardboard.

The sound of the kettle whistling broke the silence, and the children's father went back into the house and bolted the door.

Chapter Four

Rebecca Gets Out Of Her Depth.

When the children left for school that morning, their father had propped the door open so that they would not see the marks. Joe met them at the corner, and the three of them walked up the road together. Ahead of them, the church tower of Kilkhampton could be seen above the houses on the hillside that made up the village. The road was flat as it ran along the top of the valley until it reached the edge of Kilkhampton, but it was a long walk of over a mile and Rebecca began to complain.

"I'm tired!" she said crossly. "We should have told dad about last night, then we would have had a day off!"

"Why, what happened last night?" asked Joe.

Simon scowled at his sister and shook his head, "Aw nothing really. Rebecca had a nightmare, that's all."

She scowled back and replied sharply, "Oh really? That's rich isn't it! You were the one having nightmares if I recall, and anyway, I think we should tell Joe. He's our friend."

Joe stopped walking and looked up at Simon searchingly. His blonde hair wrapped tightly across his face in the wind, and he said, "What sort of nightmare?"

Simon thought about it for a second. "Can't really remember now."

Rebecca's face was already scowling and grinning at the same time. It was an expression Simon knew well. It meant she was about to do or say something mischievous.

"No that's right, he can't remember. You see when he was a baby, he slipped on a banana skin and banged his head, and ever since then he can't remember things, isn't that right Simon dear?"

Simon winced at the stupidity of her explanation, but he had no choice but to nod graciously. Joe looked at Simon sympathetically. "How unfortunate for you Simon."

Rebecca beamed at them both, and they continued along the road to school.

* * * * * * *

Back at the house the children's father worked all day sanding the deep grooves out of the door and painting it, so that when he picked them up at the end of school to bring them home, he knew there would be no trace of the damage of the previous evening.

He met Joe too, as the three of them came out of the gate together.

"This is Joe," Rebecca said proudly as she opened the door to the old Landrover.

The children's father gave a friendly smile and held out a hand, "Joe, how nice to meet you."

"Hello," said Joe shyly.

"There's plenty of room for one more if you need a lift Joe. Where do you live anyway?"

A nervous expression spread across his face and he stepped back a little.

"No really, it's alright. I prefer to walk."

"That's a pity," said Simon. "I was hoping to see where you lived so that we could come and visit you."

"Well to tell the truth I'm a little busy at the moment, but perhaps when things go quiet again I'll call round."

Rebecca puzzled over Joe's reaction for a moment. Why was he always so secretive about his home?

For most of the journey back to Stibb she thought about it, but it wasn't until she got back to the cottage that she had an idea.

She was standing in the kitchen, which overlooked the road, when she saw Joe walking past on his way home. She instinctively crouched below the sink so that she couldn't be seen, as she watched him turn down the lane towards the woodland that was opposite their house.

"Hey Simon, come and look out of the kitchen window," she called. "He must be on his way home."

But Simon didn't reply. He was playing his computer games. She watched Joe disappear round the corner of the road that led down the hill known as Iron Hill. As soon as she thought it was safe, she threw her arms into her coat and opened the freshly painted door of the cottage.

She ran to the corner in time to see Joe's back disappear into the trees on the hillside below. The hill sloped down into a valley carpeted by a blanket of green woodland trees. At the head of the valley was Kilkhampton village, and just below that was the old castle, now just a green hill. She looked down and across to where the valley ended at the beach of Duckpool. The beach was hidden, but the turquoise blue ocean stood out clearly in the 'V' shape between the hill slopes.

"It's like Dad said, there are no houses down there," Rebecca muttered to herself, but she was already moving into the edge of the road and creeping down it after Joe.

Half way down the hill, Joe turned along a muddy track that took him across a field. This led to the top of the woods. He made his way around the trees on the edge of the hill, and then turned down a narrower and very steep track that took him deep into the woodland itself.

Still behind him, Rebecca crept down the steep track. It was dark in there away from the light of the late afternoon. A slight mist moved through the trees, and only the sounds of the woodland echoed around her. As she crouched, her hands gripped the damp moss that grew against the trunk of a tree. She watched Joe leave the track for the thick cover of the woodland. Where was he going?

From a tree close by him, a fox appeared at his ankles and walked alongside him. Joe turned and crouched down to greet the fox. It put its front paws upon his leg and rubbed its face against the side of Joe's head affectionately, like a pet dog.

Rebecca was astounded, for now a bird flew from a tree and settled upon his shoulder, and a squirrel bounced along the ground towards him. Indeed the woodland came alive with animals appearing from nowhere to greet him. As he moved along, the gathering of animals moved with him, until he came to what could only be described as a narrow goalpost structure, made from logs which resembled a doorway. Small wooden carvings of animals: birds, a badger and a fox, had been placed along the top of this bizarre gateway, and creeping ivy sprawled up the posts.

Joe turned to his followers, and waving a hand towards the surrounding trees, he said, "Come my friends, you know that you may not pass through the gate. Now away to your homes."

The animals disappeared slowly into the trees. Rebecca was some twenty metres away watching them retreat into the undergrowth. She could not believe her eyes, and she wanted to call out to Joe, but now Joe turned back to the gate and passed through it. A bright, white glow flashed out from his clothing. She saw that coarsely woven trousers had replaced his jeans, and instead of his coat, he wore a thick green tunic drawn in at the waist by a black belt. He made his way down a slope through the trees, until he came to the bank of a lake. The black waters were still, and a light mist swirled forbiddingly over the top.

Rebecca passed through the gate at the top of the bank, and she stood looking down the slope at Joe's back. Then, Joe stepped out into the water and began to wade in. He was up to his waist, then his chest, and then he arched forward over the water into a dive. Rebecca saw his feet break the surface for a brief moment, and then he was gone.

She crouched still for a second, then five seconds. Five became ten, and then fifteen. What had she seen? It was too long. Why had he not come to the surface again? The water must surely be freezing! It looked black and still, and nothing stirred.

Then Rebecca began to panic. She had to do something, and in an instant she was leaping down the steep slope. A flurry of leaves cascaded down with her as she forced her way through the trees.

"Joe!" she screamed, and again, "Joe!"

A tear ran down her cheek as she stood looking out over the black still water.

"Joe!"

Nothing stirred. She stepped into the freezing waters of the lake. The cold sensation soaked through her trainers and nipped against her toes before it spread up through her jeans to her knees. The bed of the lake was soft mud, and she stepped forward again to avoid sinking. But this time she slipped and fell. There was a loud splash, and Rebecca let out a scream. She felt the cold water soaking through her clothes, making her arms heavy. She stretched out a foot to reach for the bottom but instead there was nothing there. Then she tried to strike out for the bank, but her waterlogged coat made her arms so heavy that they barely broke the water. Still more she struggled, but the cold was draining her energy from her now, and her clothes began to pull her under. She tilted her head back to gasp for air, but she was barely at the surface. The cold sensation was making her dizzy, and she fought for breath as her lips broke the surface one last time. For then she began to sink into the darkness of the lake.

Chapter Five

Joe's Secret.

Rebecca drifted silently down into the blackness of the deep water, but still she fought to get up to the surface. It was no use though; the lake had the better of her. All she saw now was the murky, cold, dark water around her.

But then she felt someone take her hand. A strange warmth spread from its clasp through her body and up into her head. It was still murky, but the black grew to a soft brown light, and then Rebecca realised, she was near to the surface of the lake once again. She looked up to see silvery bubbles rising above her to the shimmering light of day over her head. Holding her hand was the blurred shape of a boy.

The two pushed their way though the waters and broke out into the air above once more.

Rebecca spluttered. "Joe, I thought you had drowned."

Steam rose from the two of them, and Rebecca wasn't cold at all now. Joe looked at her for a moment, and then he calmly asked, "So, did you see everything?"

Rebecca smiled proudly. "Pretty much everything."

Joe wasn't swimming, but they glided over to the bank. Then they seemed to rise up out of the water to the edge of the lake, and then still holding her hand, Joe helped her to step onto the bank.

"Okay," said Joe, "let's get you home before the sun goes down."

Rebecca sat back on the slope. "Not so fast Joe," she said narrowing her eyes. "What's going on, and who or what are you!"

"Well it is a little complicated," he said smiling, "but I suppose I could start by telling you that although I look eleven, I'm actually quite a lot older. In fact I will be one thousand three hundred and twenty seven on my next birthday."

"What?" gasped Rebecca.

"Oh wait, there's more." continued Joe, but Rebecca edged up the bank a little, before interrupting again.

"Does that make you a ghost?" she asked nervously.

Joe thought for a second, it was tempting to say 'yes' just to tease her, but he thought he ought to be honest about something this important.

"No, I'm not dead, in fact I'm very much alive."

He told her the story of how many years ago he

saved the King's sword from the evil Shadow Lord, who wanted to use its magic to rule the world in eternal winter forever.

He told of how, as an eleven year old he was cornered by the lord on the shores of the lake, and how he threw the sword in and was forced to follow it.

"Like you Rebecca, I sank into the depth beneath the water, but I was saved during my dying moments by the Lady Of The Lake. She breathed life back into my lungs, and I found I could see and breathe beneath the water.

However, there was a price to pay. The magic that saved me meant I could never live again in the world of normal man. Instead I made my home with the Lady Of The Lake, who taught me the skills of swordsmanship with the sword I saved.

The lady now sleeps, and has done for a thousand years while I watch over her. The animals of the woods know me as, 'The Watcher', and whilst she sleeps and the sword is safely at my side, then the world is safe. For the Shadow Lord has been dead from this world for well over a millennium, and he lives only in dreams now. His followers tried many times to use his magic to reach the sword, so that they might release him again into the world of men, but the powerful spell of an ancient magician prevents them from crossing the threshold of the gate."

Joe paused and then continued.

"But something terrible has happened, and I am ashamed to tell you what it is, but I know I must. I am still eleven years old inside, and I missed the friendship of other children. Four hundred years ago, I used to stand in the trees near the edge of the woods where the village had grown. I could hear the playful cries and laughter of the children who lived there, and I longed to be with them. Then one day as I rested by a stream deep within the wood, I saw two children who had lost their way. For some time I watched them before I decided to leave the cover of the trees. I could see no harm in being helpful, so I went to them. We spoke of how the world had changed and I took them to the edge of the woods by the village. I soon forgot about my important job and we lay on the grass of the field talking in the midday sun. I took off the sword as it was uncomfortable, and we began to joke and laugh."

"Go on," said Rebecca.

"But then I was startled by the sound of men's voices drawing near. I ran back into the cover of the woods to avoid discovery, but in my haste I left the sword upon the bank. It was too late, and before I could go back to get it, a man had appeared and he found the children and my beloved sword. That was the last day that I saw the sword, yet I have looked for it every day since."

Rebecca could piece the rest together. "And you've started going to school because you're hoping you might find out where the sword is."

"I have the sword's jewel here in my pocket," continued Joe, "and I know that whilst it sparkles, the sword is not in the hands of the Shadow Lord's followers. But every moment could be my last. For the Shadow Lord has many followers. If he is awoken into the world of men, and he rides once again to the shores of this lake with the sword in his hand, then there will be no escape for me. The world as it is would be lost."

Rebecca sat motionless on the bank with her mouth slightly open. Her mind whirled at the possibility that the rusty old sword at her home could be the very same one that Joe was talking about. How could it be? The sword had come down from father to children in her family for generations. She remembered her fathers words, 'that old sword goes all the way back in history.' Then she thought of her dream of the golden sword, and of her brother's dream about the dark figure, and of the strange meeting with the woman.

If the woman was a follower of the Shadow Lord, then the whereabouts of the sword was already known, If that was true, they were even at that second in great danger.

She stared intensely at Joe, who was still waiting for some kind of reaction.

"So, what do you think?" he prompted.

Her face broke out into an excited smile and her eyes sparkled. She could barely contain herself, but she hardly dared to say it for fear that someone nearby might hear.

"Joe!" she whispered, "I know where it is. I know exactly where the sword is!"

Chapter Six

The Awakening.

Back at the house, Simon still sat playing on his computer games.

His dad called up the stairs. "Hey Simon, where did Rebecca say she was going?"

Simon's bike leaped over a mud bank and skidded into the lake. "Oh Dad, you made me crash now! I don't know, she didn't say," he yelled back impatiently.

"Well, I'm off to the shop to get some pasties for dinner. I'm only going to be a couple of minutes."

He pulled the door shut behind him, and walked down the path to the Landrover. But as it left Stibb village and rattled along the road towards Kilkhampton, a woman stepped out of the shadow of the trees on the opposite side of the road. She quickly crossed it and walked up the pathway to the front door.

Simon had just restarted the game when he heard the door go. He gave a heavy sigh. Either it was his sister, which meant he would get no more peace, or his father, who had forgotten something. Either way it was a nuisance. He bounded down the stairs and threw open the door.

There before him stood the woman once again. He found himself staring into her dark eyes, and his knees went weak. He wanted to step back and close the door, but it was no use. He managed to take one pace, but he felt the bottom of his foot turn cold as it touched the ground. Now he felt the cold sensation rising up his legs to his knees, then to his waist.

All the while the woman was repeating some kind of meaningless chant. Her strange words echoed into his mind and he began to dream. The dark figure from his nightmare appeared in a black mist. This time it said nothing, but the cold sensation continued to rise up Simon's body. It was up to his neck now, and he began to choke and struggle for breath. He felt faint and his mind whirled around the figure.

He wasn't sure how many seconds he was captured by the woman's spell. He remembered her sneer as she leaned over the top of him with the sword in her hand. Then she crouched down and whispered, "You will forget all that has come to pass in our meeting, now sleep for the hour is mine." Her cruel laugh cackled through the house, as a blast of wind blew into the room turning the pictures crooked on the walls, and blowing a vase off the shelf. The clock above the fire stopped, and Simon's memory of what had taken place was gone.

* * * * * * *

He came round to find that he was lying on the floor near to the open door. Rebecca leaned over him with Joe, and she was shaking him roughly by the shoulder.

"What happened?" Simon croaked out.

"Oh Simon, thank goodness you're alright! We just came back and found you like this, and the sword, it's gone!" Rebecca cried.

The three of them straightened up the room just in time for the Landrover to rattle into the driveway, and they hastily sat down to the table pretending to be relaxed as their father pushed open the door.

"Alright, feeding time at the zoo," he called out. "Oh, so you're back are you young lady? Honestly the way you fly off here, there and everywhere, it's like living with Mary Poppins, and I thought you wouldn't do this kind of thing till you were a teenager. Oh, hi Joe! Are you hungry?"

The distraction of seeing Joe prevented further discussions and their father didn't notice the missing sword, but it was a sullen meal and the children hardly spoke.

"Well, I tell you what Joe," said the children's

father as he cleared the table, "I never had it this quiet with these two. You can come any time you like if you can keep it this peaceful."

He filled the sink with water and began the washing up, and the children went up to Simon's room.

Rebecca and Joe explained the sword and Joe's presence to Simon, who listened intensely. He shared his nightmare with Joe, who was visibly upset at their incredible misfortune.

"If only I had come to your house sooner, I would have recognised the sword," said Joe.

"If only I had told you about my nightmare on the way to school this morning, you would have guessed it was the Shadow Lord," replied Simon.

Rebecca was quiet for a second, then she said, "Is there anymore stuff we don't know Joe?"

"There's plenty, but you already know more than you should," he answered cautiously.

"Joe, it's pretty obvious now that you need our help. You can't hope to get back the sword without us. You need us," insisted Simon.

"That may be true, but you and I are from different worlds," said Joe. "It is too dangerous for you, and this isn't a game. The Shadow Lord was once a man, but his mind was taken over by his selfish thoughts. He killed many noble knights for his own gain. If the sword is used to awaken him to this world once more, he will ride in battle again. With the sword in his hand he will be unstoppable."

* * * * * * *

A lonely house stood on a cliff top four miles away. Far beneath it, the ocean waves crashed against the rocks at the base of the cliff, and the north winds raced across the water and whistled round the eaves of the house.

Inside the house was an empty upstairs room. A fire burned in the grate, but there was no other light. No pictures hung from the plain walls, and the fire's flicker reflected against the shining planks of the floor.

The woman stood alone in the centre of the room with the sword at her feet, its tip pointing to the fire. She whispered the words of an ancient spell, and the fire began to flicker and grow. The waves pushed harder against the bottom of the cliff outside, washing higher up the stone face with each line she uttered. The sound of the wind steadily intensified, and still she poured out the words.

The fire was blazing now, its flames reaching out into the room like the talons of a beast. The ocean pounded the cliff, stretching further and further up to the house. It was as if the arms of lost souls were reaching out of their watery graves, hoping to grab onto something that might offer salvation, and the wind became a roar.

Still she continued to weave the spell against the blaze of the fire. Figures began to appear through the flames, and dark shadow-like forms stepped out into the room, lining up along either wall. Their almost transparent grey bodies could barely be seen in the dim light, but they were as tall as men if rather twig-like in appearance. Rough jagged edges of wrinkled, grey skin hung from every spidery limb and the lines of their jaws. Hair sprouted in tufts from their narrow pointed heads, and thick eyebrows dangled over their yellow eyes. Some had mouths that gaped open, whilst others seemed to have no mouth at all.

Then from deep within the dancing flames a solid form began to appear. Suddenly the wind drew its breath back, and there was a moment of terrible stillness. The figures around the room were drawn back into the fire, and it roared so powerfully that the woman cried out. Then the wind returned to its normal whistle and the fire burned steadily. A black shape stood in front of the fire. It cast its shadow across the room and onto the woman.

She looked at the shrouded silhouette. It was of human form, though no features could be seen, for it was in shadow. Only the drapes of a long, black cape and sinister cowl, that concealed the monstrous glaring eyes beneath, seemed solid enough to touch.

The Shadow Lord was back in the world of men.
On the floor before him lay the sword that was the
key to all he could hope to aspire to.

* * * * * * *

Back in Simon's room, Joe fumbled for the jewel in his pocket. He pulled it out into the light of the room.

"Oh no!" he gasped. "Look at the jewel. The sparkle has gone!"

In his hand he clutched a small oval stone. As the children peered deeply into it, they saw its centre becoming dark and misted. The darkness seemed to be spreading outwards, and was as black as coal.

* * * * * * *

In the room of the lonely house on the cliff, the Shadow Lord paced angrily up and down on the varnished floor.

"The sword is incomplete," he shouted. "It is useless to me without the jewel in the centre." His rage intensified. "Now where is it?"

"My lord," replied the woman in a quivering, soft voice. "I did my best to serve you well. I knew nothing of the jewel. Please spare me so that we can go to the house where I found the sword. There are two children there. They will know where the jewel is."

The Shadow Lord's white eyes widened. He

remembered the child that thwarted him of the sword many centuries ago. That child would have been dead for over a thousand years, but he remembered his rage when the sword was cast out over the waters of the lake. His eyes narrowed, for he hated all children, with the bitterness of a thousand years. It was a hatred that twisted into his black, lifeless heart.

"Two children you say?" he said ponderingly. "Then let us away, so that I may crush them into dust."

Chapter Seven

Nelleth And Zilef.

The three children sat facing each other on the floor in Simon's bedroom. Simon held the stone in his fingers. He looked deep into the dark centre.

"I don't get it," he said, "why isn't the jewel still in the sword anyway?"

"Well, the problem was, that when the jewel was in place, the magic was too strong for me. It was dangerous! All sorts of things happen when the jewel is in the sword, but without it the sword is only half its real power," said Joe.

Rebecca began to smile.

"What's so funny Rebecca?" said Simon crossly.

Rebecca grinned even more. "Well I just had this thought," she said. "If the sword is only half its power without the jewel then why should it be any different for the Shadow Lord? I mean just imagine how cross you would be if you were him, and you found yourself back in our world, with the sword, but it didn't work because of the missing jewel."

"Oh my!" gasped Joe. "She's right! He won't be

able to use its magic without the jewel." He leapt to his feet. "Okay, now for some more stuff that I never told you. I have an idea. I have these two friends down in the woods......."

Rebecca interrupted. "Are they animals?"

"Well sort of, but then, not exactly. I have to go and see them alone though because, well, they are a bit stubborn sometimes. You two keep the Jewel and I'll go and see them straight away. In the mean time, act normally till I come back to you."

Rebecca held out her hand to Simon who still had the jewel in his fingers. He frowned but passed it to her without argument, because bossy as she was, she wouldn't lose it. She pushed it into her pocket. "There, now it will be safe." she said.

The children took Joe to the door of the cottage and opened it to the black night air.

" See you directly," said Joe.

"But you'll need a torch," said Simon.

Joe smiled. "No I won't," he said confidently. Part of the lake's magic meant that he could see his way in the dark better than an owl. The children's vision was shrouded by the blanket of night, but Joe could see every leaf on every tree. He saw a shrew inching its way through the grass in the garden, and a badger that picked its way across the field in the distance.

The children walked with him as far as the gate at the end of the path. Then they watched his back disappear into the night, as he made his way to the road that led down Iron Hill into the woods. They stood still for a second, staring into the darkness before turning back to the house. In the distance a rumble of thunder sounded out across the night sky.

Down in the woods the moisture dripped from the leaves around Joe as he made his way through the trees. He moved with the stealth of a wild animal, planting his feet silently between the slippery tree roots that twisted and knotted along the woodland floor. He moved through the wet leaves and twigs with such light-footedness that he made no sound. For this was Joe's world and he was the master of it.

Eventually he came upon a long dried up riverbed. For ten more minutes he crept silently along it until he stopped. Some way up the bank there was a group of large tunnels, each was around one square metre, and led a long way back into the darkness. Tree roots hung from the roof of a tunnel as he peered cautiously inside. It bore some testimony to the size of a creature that would make a hole so large to nest in, and Joe knew that he should take care not to startle the dwellers that might be within the lair.

"Nelleth, Zilef, are you there?" he called softly, but there was no reply.

A loud cracking noise through the trees some two hundred metres away caused Joe to turn swiftly. He caught sight of a giant set of back legs and a tail disappearing into the undergrowth. Joe crept forward into a clearing where the beast had gone, and there in front of him were two dragons.

Each stood at shoulder height but they were up to three metres long. At the end of their powerful legs were hand-like feet with long black claws. Thick muscular necks supported large, square heads with dark, piercing eyes and rounded nostrils. Their forked tongues shot out and recoiled swiftly every so often to taste the air. A thick chain-mail of scaly grey skin, scarred from battle, but tough enough to withstand attack, stretched tightly over their backs. Tucked in at their shoulder blades were their wings, which were wrapped so tightly against them that they were barely visible.

Nelleth looked at Joe somewhat crossly and stamped one foot before she spoke.

"We've been waiting ages for you to come to see us, Watcher. You've seen everyone else in the woods twice, but we always have to wait!"

Nelleth was over five thousand years old, yet in dragon years she was only around seven. Joe smiled affectionately.

"I'm sorry Nelleth. I must say your wings are growing beautifully."

Her eyelids fluttered and she spread them out proudly for Joe to see.

"Do you know how long I have waited for my wings to grow?" she said. "It took two thousand years, that's twenty four thousand months, or a hundred and four thousand weeks, or even seven hundred and twenty thousand days."

"Wow, your maths is better too!" said Joe.

"Not really. I didn't work it out, I just counted."

Zilef, her brother moved forward.

"And how are you Zilef?" asked Joe.

"Oh, all right, I suppose. I'm a bit bored though. I've done my best to think of something to do, but I just can't think of anything!"

Zilef was a similar age to his sister, but he couldn't be bothered to count so he wasn't sure exactly how old he was.

"Okay, now listen," said Joe, "I've come to talk to you about the sword. I really need your help."

Nelleth drew in a breath, "Oh, watch out, I think I'm going to, Ah.. Ah.. Ah.. Ahchooooo!!!!!"

A ball of flames shot from Nelleth's mouth. Joe dived out of the way just in time, but the fire caught his boot, which smouldered, releasing a small trail of smoke as he picked himself up.

Zilef began to titter, trying desperately not to laugh.

"Do excuse me," said Nelleth sarcastically, "I'm dreadfully sorry."

"Now please you two, I really need your help. The Shadow Lord is back in the world of men and there isn't much time".

* * * * * * *

Back at the cottage in Stibb, the children's father was asleep by the fire. The children had gone to bed, but they remained in their clothes in case Joe should return before morning.

The first streaks of lightning cracked across the black night sky overhead and lit up the garden of the cottage beneath, as the black-cloaked arm of the Shadow Lord reached out to the door. He had no need even to touch it, for the latch flew back, and the door swung slowly open to the room inside.

He stood in the room over the children's sleeping father, and waved a hand over his head and whispered. "Sleep!"

Then he crossed to the stairs and began to climb them.

Simon was soundly sleeping in his room, as was Rebecca in hers, with the jewel still in her pocket. They were totally unaware of the figure rounding the top of the stairs and moving across to Simon's door.

Chapter Eight

The Storm Over Roughtor.

The figure waved a hand across Simon's face, and then lifted him from the bed. He was taken down the stairs and out into the night, where the woman was waiting in an old, green car.

Once again the figure climbed the stairs and he moved towards the door of Rebecca's room. In the darkness inside she stirred, for she was too hot with all her clothes on. She opened her eyes too late. The Shadow Lord stood over her with his arm outstretched. She drew in a breath to scream, but as she did so, the powerful sleeping magic worked its spell, and she sighed and was asleep once more.

* * * * * * *

Back in the woods, Joe had just about completed his story. "So you see, I need you to help me. Zilef, I want you to come with me to the cottage, to collect Simon and Rebecca. Nelleth, I would like you to circle the skies looking for anything unusual that might tell where the sword may be."

Nelleth raised her two front legs from the ground.

She spread her mighty wings, and shot a tower of fire into the sky. "I *will* find your sword, young Watcher. You can count on me."

There was a sudden rush of air upon the ground as she beat her wings, and with a flick of her tail, she lifted from the ground and was gone into the night.

Zilef trotted forward two steps, "Get on my back then, so we can go," he said.

Joe took a step back. "Is it safe?"

"Of course it's safe!"

He placed his hand against the dragon's tough, dry scales, and then he leapt onto Zilef's back.

"Now hold tight! I'm not much good at taking off," the dragon yelled out.

"You're what?" stammered Joe.

But the dragon pushed hard from the ground with his legs. He spread his wings high above Joe's head and pulled them down around his body. Joe hardly dared to look as they lifted from the ground in the clearing and over the top of the trees. The dragon again stretched his wings out and thrust them down. With every thrust, the two were lifted higher into the sky, until the clearing was just a small circle far below them. Then they soared over the trees and above the fields, towards the lights of Stibb.

They circled the village and the dragon swooped

low over the roofs of the little cottages near the road, lifting his feet to avoid tall chimneys and telegraph poles. Then he stretched out his wings to slow their descent and they touched gently down in the road outside the children's cottage.

"Quickly into the skies again and wait for me there," said Joe. "If someone sees you in the road they might die of fright!"

The dragon disappeared into the air once more and Joe crept into the garden of the cottage. As he approached the door, he could see that it was still open. He stepped inside and there was the children's father, deeply asleep.

Something was wrong. He hurried up the stairs to Simon's room, but it was empty. Hastily he made his way into Rebecca's room, but that was empty too.

He remembered the jewel that he had left in the two children's care. If that should fall into the hands of the Shadow Lord, then all would be lost.

He raced back down the stairs and out into the garden, calling into the air.

"Zilef, come quickly, there's something wrong, they're gone! We must find them!"

* * * * * * *

The dark Shadow Lord and his sneering accomplice stood on the top of a hill known as Roughtor. Large oval boulders worn smooth by the weather were stacked up above their heads. A fire blazed in a circle of stones, and on a flat slab lay the sleeping children. Simon was first to wake. He opened his eyes and found Rebecca still sleeping next to him.

"Wake up!" snarled the Shadow Lord.

Rebecca woke with a startled jump. In the dark figure's hand flashed the sword, but it was different. It looked new and was shining in its full splendour.

"Now I have the sword, and that makes me a god!" roared the hooded one.

Loose pebbles and shale tumbled from the surrounding rocks, and a streak of lightning flashed in the sky above the figure's head. The children huddled together and began to tremble at the deep, hollow voice that shook the very ground beneath their feet.

"Now," the figure continued in a quieter voice, "tell me where the jewel is, and pray that I like your answer or it will be your last!" His white eyes flashed beneath the cowl that concealed his face.

Both remained silent. His voice came like thunder into their ears.

"Answer me!"

He crouched down to Rebecca with the sword pointed at her.

"Don't you dare touch her!" cried Simon with rage.

But now the figure turned his white eyes upon Simon. Simon's words died in his throat and he felt weak with fear. The Shadow Lord grabbed hold of him by the shoulder, and he was seized with such a strong grip that he winced. He was lifted from the ground, and his feet kicked at the air as he struggled to shake himself free.

Then the figure began to chant strange words. The fire flared up and gruesome dark shapes of men stepped from the flames, as they had before in the lonely house. They began to swirl in a black whirlwind through the air around the Shadow Lord and the boy.

But at that moment, through the fire, came the dragon Nelleth. She sent logs hurtling over the ground and a shower of red sparks into the air. This was not the Nelleth of the woods, for now she faced her darkest adversary. The edges of her mouth drew back into a contorted snarl, revealing her white pointed teeth. Her talons were curled and her furious eyes were upon the group.

Simon had been flung upon the ground in a moment of confusion during her entrance, but the Shadow Lord was quick to compose himself. He turned and raised the sword to the dragon. The two children had no idea that Nelleth was a friend, and they trembled even more at the sight of her in her battling majesty, for never before had they seen a dragon.

Nelleth roared at the Shadow Lord, and a fury of tumbling flames blasted through the dark shapes that had come from the fire.

"What have we here?" laughed the Shadow Lord, "a baby dragon? You are no match for me, for this is the sword you may never fight against. Your very life is mine whilst I hold it!"

Nelleth leapt forward at the Shadow Lord, and with a swipe of her talons, she tore through the black robe across his chest. The Shadow Lord cried out in pain and placed a hand to the wound, but then the sword flashed through the air as the two did battle.

The blows of the sword glanced from Nelleth's claws but sank deeply into her skin. Wildly, she struck out at the hooded one with all her strength, and again and again the night sky was lit up, as from deep within her, she forced a rage of flames against her adversary.

At the beginning of the fight, it looked as if she would win as she swung her claws ferociously, but slowly, he pushed her back. Her fire was gone and so was her strength. She slipped and stumbled, exhausted from the battle. The children watched in horror, as the Shadow Lord raised the sparkling blade into the air above her wing.

"You knew you could not stand against the sword!" he laughed. Then he growled with anger, and brought the sword down upon her wing with such violence that it cut straight through.

Nelleth screamed out in pain, as her beautiful wing was severed and fell limply upon the ground. The children gasped in horror at her injury, while the Shadow Lord crossed to her other side.

"Dragons have always been the objects of hate for men. Why would you want to save two children when you knew you could never win?"

He brought the sword down upon the other wing. Again she screamed in pain, and a tear came from her eye as the other wing slipped from her side onto the ground. Simon and Rebecca stood motionless until this moment.

"Simon, we have to do something, he's killing her!" sobbed Rebecca.

Simon was frantic to help, but he could see no way of preventing the Shadow Lord from his evil deed. The Shadow Lord held the sword close to the dragon and was still taunting her, but then he plunged it into the earth near her head while he walked round her.

There it was. A moment of hope as the sword stood unguarded upon the open ground. Something about the sparkling metal upon the blade seized Simon's attention, and he found himself standing captivated by its beauty. A strange sensation, almost like warmth, began to spread through him and he felt his arms rising from his sides and reaching forward. The further he reached towards the sword, the more his courage grew within him; suddenly what needed to be done was clear.

"Now is our chance!" he yelled, and he sprinted across the ground to the sword. The figure turned and lunged at him, but he had just enough time to hurl the sword towards Rebecca before he was seized. Simon was dropped to the ground as the figure turned swiftly towards the girl.

"Run Becca, run!" Simon yelled.

Rebecca leapt from the flat stone, and raced off down the hill into the night.

"After her!" commanded the hooded one, and the man-like shapes from the flames, the woman, and the figure moved in an incredulous frenzy of leaping and shouting, swiftly into the night after Rebecca.

Simon stood alone facing the dragon. She spoke softly. "I won't harm you. I was sent to find the sword by the Watcher, but I saw you in danger and thought I could help. Oh my beautiful wings! All my life I have waited for my wings to grow, counting each day until I could reach into the sky." Another tear fell from her eye to the ground.

"Look at you, you're bleeding!" said Simon. He looked hastily around him, "We should go. They might come back."

His eyes twinkled. Slowly he stretched out a trembling hand to the creature and stroked her scaly skin. "Can you stand?" he asked.

The dragon pulled herself to her feet, and the two of them left the hilltop.

* * * * * * *

Down on the hillside, Rebecca stumbled over rocks and through watery marshes. The heavy sword glistened in the dark. Behind her she could hear the strange sound of the shadow men squelching over the ground. Her blood throbbed through her veins and her breathless lungs gasped ever more for rest, but still she raced on.

She entered a narrow gap between two walls of rock and went along it for a few seconds. Then she came to a stop, for it was a dead end, and she was faced by a sheer rock that rose out beyond her view.

Quickly she spun round to retreat along the passageway, but she was too late and the squelching feet drew ever near. Through the darkness, she began to make out the vague outline of the men as they drew closer. They were so close that she heard the hiss of their whispering voices. She thought of the jewel in her pocket and she looked down to the sword that she held in her hand. The shapes moved clearly towards her. Rebecca was trapped.

Chapter Nine

Nelleth's Final Stand.

Rebecca frantically looked around her. She found herself wishing that she could be anywhere except the narrow passage of rock that she was trapped in. Then her gaze caught sight of a strange glow within her pocket. It was the jewel.

She thrust her hand in and pulled it out. It was radiating light from within its centre. As she watched it flickering in her hand she had an idea. She could put the jewel into the sword and try to use the magic.

In the back of her mind she remembered Joe telling her and Simon that the magic was too strong, and it was dangerous, but if she did nothing the sword and jewel would be taken, and all would be lost. Without a second thought she pushed the stone in. Immediately the sword began to resonate with a strange low humming sound. The light coming from the jewel grew to a blinding dazzle, and the shadow men, who had moved forward to seize Rebecca, were forced to cower back with their eyes covered. Rebecca held both hands around the sword's handle and pointed it out towards the encroaching men.

'If only I were as big as you,' she thought, 'If only I were skilled enough to fight you like a grown up!'

A bolt of pain shot through Rebecca. Her knees, wrists, ankles and back began to ache, and her scalp itched furiously. She began to feel strange tingles and twitches within her muscles.

"Oh," she groaned, "what's happening to me?"

Her hair began to sprout from her head and cascade in long, thick curls down past her shoulders. She looked down to see the ground moving further away, and the sword began to feel strangely lighter.

There was a sudden flash from the jewel, and Rebecca found herself dressed in a suit of golden armour up to the neck. She felt strong and swift, and could sense the movements of the shadow men around her. Her blood raced through her veins, not with exhaustion anymore, but with thrill at the thought of battle, and with a cry of vengeance, she jumped high into the air and landed in amongst the shadow people.

Again and again she swung the sword, cutting her way through the crowd of dark shapes as if they were thistles in a field. She possessed lightning speed and deadly accuracy. The cries of the dying shapes as they vanished into dust filled the air around her, and some began to turn and run, but there was no escape for them and she somersaulted over their heads, so that they were cut off in the passageway themselves. There were four in all. Three charged at her and she cut them down with one mighty blow. Now only one shape stood before her.

"Now listen to me!" she said calmly. "You tell the Shadow Lord that I have the sword now, and I *will* return it to the Watcher." She stepped aside and the lonely shape ran off into the night.

Rebecca stood and looked down at herself. She was tall and strong. Her hands had long, slender, delicate fingers, and she reached up to touch her curly dark hair.

"I don't believe it," she gasped, "I'm a grown up! Boy I'm going to be in trouble when mum finds out!"

She ran out of the gap in between the rocks and onto the moors that covered the side of the hill.

* * * * * * *

Nelleth led Simon along through the dark.

"We have to reach Rocky Valley," she said. "From there we can go by sea to the beach at Duckpool. That part will be dangerous, for Duckpool is a dark place. The sword's magic will be of no use for it is the stronghold of great misfortune. We must take care, but we can enter Stowe Wood through the stream to get to the lake."

Through the darkness towards them came the sound of a human's running footsteps, and both of them stopped and fearfully waited. Simon hesitantly called out. "Rebecca is that you!"

"Er, well yes, sort of." came the reply from the dark.

"Quick, we're over here. Thank goodness you're alright."

Rebecca's voice sounded thoughtful. "Well I'm not hurt, but I wouldn't exactly say I'm alright." With that Rebecca came into view of her brother.

"Who are you?" he said.

"It's me, Rebecca!" Her face was a sort of a grin and a scowl at the same time. Her 'mischief face', and Simon instantly recognised it.

"Wow!" he exclaimed. "But you're so tall, and you're different. You look a bit like Mum."

Rebecca twisted her face up. "Ew, yuk, stop it or I'll throw up!" she said.

"I don't get it, you're a grown up, look at that armour, and your hair."

"The hair, that's nothing, you wait and see what I can do with this sword!" Rebecca boasted, and she told the two of them her story.

* * * * * * *

Up on the hill top the news of the defeat and escape had reached the Shadow Lord. He clenched his fists with rage as the anger welled up within him, and at that moment, he wished that he could fire his black heart high above the heads of those who opposed him, so that it could fall back down to earth as a shower of white-hot burning sparks. He looked at the woman follower who had brought him back into the world. She had done nothing that was of any use to him, and he no longer needed her. "You, come here!" he commanded. "I have a job for you."

"What is it Sire? Just tell me so that I may carry out your bidding!" She felt a sharp jolt within her, and she gave a sudden cry and fell upon her hands and knees. She saw that her skin began to ripple unnaturally across her hand, and it began to alter in shape to that of an animal's claws. Jet-black hairs began to shoot through her skin. She let out another cry; only this time it was the roar of a panther.

The Shadow Lord gave a wicked laugh. "Your coat is of the blackest night. You are more powerful than any beast upon these moors. You can run like the wind and can strike silently. Now go and carry out my bidding. Take vengeance upon my enemies, and bring me the sword.

The panther roared and bounded out onto the moors to seek out the dark Shadow Lord's opponents.

He stood watching her for a moment, and then he turned and gazed into the flames of the fire.

"Now rise my brothers," he whispered. "Rise all the vengeance that boils within me. Rise all the selfish thoughts. Rise all the hatred of others. Rise all the war that man can bring against himself, and kneel before your master."

A dark smoke poured up from the fire, and the figures of hundreds of shadow men swirled out of it and into the air above the hill. More and more flooded out so that they ran like a river into the night sky. Hundreds became a thousand, and then two thousand. Their angry and selfish cries filled the air as they jostled to stand in rows around their hooded leader.

Next from deep within the fire, came a most unearthly cry that was neither man nor beast. The scream of air raid sirens, the sound of marching troops, the crackle of gunfire, the explosion of bombs, and the blood curdling cries of the millions of men who had died in battle since time began. Out of the fire galloped a giant creature. Its head was that of a bull on the body of a man, and it reared up on the back legs of a horse.

A silence fell upon the motley crowd as they awaited their instructions.

* * * * * * *

Down on the moors, Rebecca, Simon and the dragon had made good ground. They picked their way through the stones and crossed a small stream. The coast, and Rocky valley was less than a mile away. Nelleth struggled forward. Her breathing was shallow and quick.

"Not far to the valley," she panted. The wounds on her haunches, where her beautiful wings once were, glistened with blood that trickled down the sides of her body onto the ground.

Simon could see that she was in a lot of pain. "We're going to make it," he said. "Why don't you rest for a second."

The dragon slumped down onto a patch of grass. She turned her large head to face Simon, and tasted the air near him with her forked tongue. "I liked it when you stroked me up on the hill top," she sighed. "Why are dragons so hated by men?"

"I don't hate dragons," said Simon, "I never even knew they existed. I never met a dragon before."

"How can humans not like a thing they do not know about? Why must they mistrust a dragon when they do not even know she exists?"

A tear rolled down Simon's cheek. He had always thought that Knights were brave to do battle with dragons, and yet he had never stopped to ask himself why they were fighting.

"I'm so sorry," he said, and he put his arms around the dragon's neck and hugged her.

Rebecca stood silently watching. The dragon had saved them, and in so doing, she had lost her most precious wings and would never fly again, so that the children and the sword could be free. She placed a hand upon Simon's shoulder, and speaking bravely, but with a quiver in her voice, she said, "Come on Nelleth, let's get you into the valley. We should move on."

"Please come near me," said Nelleth softly, "so that I may look upon you with the sword in your hand." Rebecca stepped forward with the golden sword, its jewel shining powerfully. "One of the silver dragons is me," she whispered proudly. "I once stood with the king who held it in battle, and his strength was a dragon's strength, his mind was as pure and good as a dragon's mind, and he and I were the same. Now Rebecca, I have stood with you and Simon in this battle. When you look upon the silver dragons that shine upon the blade, remember your friend Nelleth, and do what you know is right. Now promise me that you will get the sword to the Watcher."

"I promise," said Rebecca, "but we will all get safely to the Watcher together. Once we get to the Rocky Valley things will be fine."

Nelleth drew in a sharp breath. "Alas I won't be coming to the Rocky Valley with you. There is a special way for me to go where humans cannot walk. You must go on without me from here. I can help you no more than this."

"But you can barely walk!" said Simon.

"It is not far," answered Nelleth. "Now go!"

Simon turned to Rebecca. He was confused, Nelleth had not mentioned this other way until now. He saw a single tear fall from Rebecca's eye. It ran down the chest plate of her golden armour, leaving a trail that glistened in the light that shone from the jewel in the sword.

"Come on Simon, we have to go," she said bravely. They turned and walked silently away across the grey moors towards the coast.

* * * * * * *

Nelleth sat still for a second, for she knew she would never see the light of day, or the sword again. Then she raised herself from the ground, for she could see movements creeping in a circle around her through the darkness. She arched her back in anger and lifted her head to let out a mighty roar. She would not lie down gently and die this night. She snarled menacingly at the shadowy forms that edged ever close to her, and in a second she was ripping her way through them with all her anger, all her hope, and with the full knowledge that this hour was her last.

In amongst them she came against the panther. It sunk its teeth deep into the wounds upon her back. In agony now she continued to slash at the air before her. She seized the panther and threw it to the ground, ripping and tearing into its flesh with her claws as it gripped her neck and began to squeeze the life from her.

Still she fought on, but the shadow people came forward by the hundred now, and as fast as she struck them down, another would take up the fight. They climbed upon her back, and they pulled with their spidery fingers at her wounds to open them up so that blood gushed from them draining her life from her.

Then she slumped upon the ground too weak to move. Before her lay the lifeless form of the black panther, and for a second, the shadow people moved back in a circle, awaiting her next move.

In her mind, she pictured Rebecca holding the sword, and she thought of the promise that she had made. A tear rolled down Nelleth's face, not out of sorrow, but out of joy, for in her last moment she saw the sword shining in Rebecca's hand. On its blade, the brilliant glare of a silver dragon, and then she was dead.

Her body dissolved into a sparkling frost upon the ground and vanished into the soil, and the crowd of figures moved away.

Chapter Ten

The Narrow Escape.

High up in the sky, Joe sat upon Zilef's back. They had gone from Stibb to the edge of the cliffs at the beach called Sandymouth, where the Atlantic Ocean started. From there they skimmed the deep, heaving waters, searching the rocky coves and clefts as far as Marsland Mouth, where Cornwall became Devon. They flew back along the steep and winding cliff paths, searching the fields and valleys, before they again left the land to search the headlands of the south towards Tintagel.

Having found nothing, they turned inland once more to search the tors and rocky outcrops of Bodmin moor. They landed on the tor next to Roughtor, to rest for a brief moment, where they were astonished to witness the dark Shadow Lord's armies rise from the fire into the sky, and sweep down across the lowlands towards the sea.

They had no idea that the armies were pursuing Simon and Rebecca who had the sword, or that at that very moment, the two children were climbing down into Rocky Valley that led to the ocean.

So they had decided to follow the Shadow Lord and

his armies until he came to rest, and then they would steal the sword somehow, and rescue the children.

At the moment of Nelleth's death, Zilef suddenly stopped, a twist of emotion shuddered within him and he knew. He lifted his head to the night air, and cried out at the lightning that flashed in the skies above.

"My poor Nelleth!" he sobbed, "What a terrible storm rages inside my mind."

"Zilef whatever is wrong?" asked Joe.

"Nelleth the most brave and noble dragon is now dead." He sat back and cried as the thunder rumbled ever closer.

* * * * * * *

At the top of the Rocky Valley the Shadow Lord stopped. He knew he could not step into the valley, as it was the sleeping place of an ancient magic that would destroy him in an instant. He growled with frustration as he saw the outline of Simon and Rebecca moving through the trees on the pathway below him, but then he turned to his followers.

"They must not reach the lake!" he said angrily. In his mind he remembered the pursuit in the wood of the small boy when last the sword escaped him. "This time I will be the victor," he muttered to himself. "Now let us go ahead to the woods of Stowe over land, where we will plan how to trap those thieves, as they run through the night into my open arms."

* * * * * * *

Rebecca and Simon crept along a muddy track that was next to a bubbling stream. Large rocks made natural steps for them to climb down. They went further into the valley where the trees became quite thick, and then they rested for a second where the water tumbled off a shelf of rock into a pool beneath. Steep forest slopes rose above them on either side, and creepers of ivy hung from branches around them. Rebecca dipped her cupped hand into the pool of water and scooped some up to drink.

"This place feels peaceful," said Simon. He looked around at the walls of rock and wet moss that twinkled in the light shining from the jewel in the sword.

Barely visible in the dim glow, he noticed a strange pattern carved into the rock. At its centre the pattern resembled a sword. Circles looped from it all the way around into a group of lines that reminded Simon of a puzzle book maze. Next to it was a second pattern that looked exactly like the first, only this time instead of a sword, Simon saw the shape of a woman with her arms out.

"Hey Rebecca, look at this. See, this one looks like the sword, and this one looks like a woman, like you."

Rebecca wasn't listening.

"Simon," she said, "Now that we're here, how are we supposed to get to Duckpool using the sea. I mean this would lead to the ocean down here," she said gesturing to the track, "but what do we do when we get there. We haven't got a boat, and even if we had one, we wouldn't want to be out in it in the dark. Not in this storm!"

Simon looked back at the other pattern. It didn't

look like a sword anymore, now it seemed to look more like a horse.

"That's odd," he said. "Come and look at these patterns!"

She came over and held the sword closer so that the patterns could be more clearly seen in the light from the jewel.

"They are pretty," she said, "but I don't see how admiring these funny patterns is going to solve our problems. Maybe there's a beach down here that we can walk along." They left the pool and moved off down the track towards the ocean.

* * * * * * *

On the open moor, Joe and Zilef had decided to take to the skies once more. They had seen that the dark army had changed its direction, and so Joe was clambering up onto the dragon's back, when across the hill in front of them galloped a large sinister shape. Its black hooves rumbled over the ground to rival the thunder in the skies. Its thick-set human shoulders swung its arms powerfully through the air, and its bull's face snorted from its flared, dripping nostrils, as it charged, horns down, through the moor land wastes.

Joe stepped down to take a closer look and turning to Zilef he said, "What evil form of magic is this?"

Zilef recognised the creature. "It is the darkest of the Shadow Lord's whisperers. The one that sleeps in all men's minds, the one that claims it can destroy the world. It is the war that man can bring against himself!"

The ghastly shape stopped and sniffed the air. Then it turned to face the boy and the dragon.

"Quickly climb up onto my back so that we can escape!" cried Zilef.

Joe stood caught by the creature's stare.

"But I can beat him!"

"How can you, you have no sword. Quickly, we must escape!" came the dragon's urgent response.

The creature stamped a foot and began to race across the open ground towards the boy.

"Please!" cried the dragon. "He is poisoning your mind with pride to fight him. He has you under his spell. We must escape. Only with the sword of truth can you strike him down."

But still the boy stood fast, stupefied by the sound of guns and bombs, as the ugly creature swept across the open ground before him. Zilef was quick to think. He seized Joe in his grip, and plucked him into the air just in time before the creature could charge him down, but it reached up and seized the dragon's tail, and began to pull him back to earth. The dragon blew down on to the monster's arm with a shower of flames, and then it let go. Zilef soared away from the ground still clutching Joe tightly.

"I don't know what came over me!" stammered Joe. "I had the strangest feeling that I would win easily, even though I knew I couldn't. I didn't care about how much I got hurt, or what would happen to me, I just wanted to stand there!"

"Only with the sword of truth will you strike him down," repeated the dragon. "Knowing when it is right to fight and when it isn't, was never part of the creature called war that man brings against himself!"

* * * * * * *

Simon and Rebecca rounded the last few rocks at the bottom of the valley where the stream joined the sea. They stood on a single black ledge that was ten feet above the breaking waves.

"Oh no, that's torn it," cried Simon.

There was no beach, no boat, and the ocean waves crashed wilfully against the edge of the rock beneath them.

"We'll have to go back," said Rebecca, and she looked back up the path.

"That's no good, they could be waiting for us just

along the track. I don't understand," said Simon exasperatedly.

The two of them looked out to the rolling waves, as the white water tumbled over itself. Large sections of foam surged forwards, sending spray back into the air in an arch, and within the arch, a familiar shape began to stir.

Chapter Eleven

The White Sea Horses Of The Waves.

The arch of spray moved as the wind blew across it like a wisp of hair, and from the turbulent wall of water that surged towards the children, broke the head of a magnificent white horse. Its front hooves danced across the froth in a shower of spray as it emerged from the breaking wave. Then from behind it came a second horse as pure and milky as the first. Together they raced forward across the surface of the water and leapt upon the rocky ledge.

Never before had Rebecca seen such an animal, its white coat, smoothed by the water, stretched tightly across its well-defined muscles. Its hooves had the appearance of pearl, and a long, white mane of silk hung from its strong neck.

"I don't believe it!" gasped Rebecca, and she glanced down to the sword. Its jewel sparkled brightly. She stretched out her hand to smooth down the horse's soft, white coat. "Where could such beautiful horses have come from?"

Simon stared thoughtfully before he commented. "They're so large!" He remembered standing on a cliff above a beach, looking out over the rough sea on a winter day, and he recalled his father asking him if he could see the white horses in the waves. "I see them," he whispered under his breath.

Rebecca spoke to break his silent memory. "Come on, I'll help you up."

"But Rebecca I can't ride a horse, let alone one this big."

In truth, the only time Rebecca had ever been on a horse was when she was led sitting on one's back around a field at a school Summer Fete, but she was determined not to let on to Simon that she was as daunted by the challenge as he was. "It's easy," she retorted confidently. "It's the same as riding a bike!"

Simon frowned, "It doesn't look like a bike, are

you sure we'll be alright?"

"I think we just have to climb up and hope for the best."

"Well where will we go? We can't go back along the pathway."

Rebecca was getting a little frustrated. "We have no other choice but to see where the horses take us. Maybe the pictures you saw in the patterns were trying to tell us that the horses were for us. Now lets get up!"

The horses stood and waited while Rebecca helped Simon up. He gripped the mane in his fingers marvelling at its soft texture. Rebecca hauled herself up onto her horse's back. She sat up straight in her golden armour and raised the sword. "Hey Simon, how do I look?" she asked.

"Like a princess," he replied nervously.

Barely had Rebecca gripped her steed's mane, when the two horses leapt from the rock and out over the water. She and Simon wailed in disbelief as they streaked out over the wash picking up incredible speed. With their riders screaming on their backs, out and further out they charged, towards the enormous crashing waves. At the last moment when Simon thought the rolling wave would hit him, his horse leapt up and over the turbulent waters that tumbled frantically before him, and galloped on towards the next mighty hurdle, that raised itself from the depth beneath.

The cold wind rushed against his clothes, pinning them tightly to his arms, thighs and chest, and causing any loose trailing material to flap wildly as he raced into the night. The powerful onrush of air forced its way into his half open mouth, so that it was difficult to breathe without turning sideways, and his eyes streamed.

Occasional chop caught the horses' hooves and sent spray flying into the rider's faces, stinging their eyes and blinding them. By Simon's side, Rebecca was enjoying the exhilaration of the chase, as the two white horses breached the gap in the waves for the open ocean. Now they turned and charged along the coastline, north-bound towards Stowe.

Sometimes they leapt clear of the water completely as they rose up over the mighty ocean swells, and other times they dipped to their knees thrashing through the rises and troughs of the unbroken waves.

Upon the land to the right, the two riders passed the lights of the small towns and havens, that stood out against the silhouette of the cliffs and the inland reaches behind.

On reaching the shores of Sandymouth, the horses leapt clear of the rocks that ran outwards into the ocean like fences to fields, and they powered along the rocky base of the cliff until they reached the shores of Duckpool at the bottom of Stowe Valley.

The horses rounded the final bend in the rocks and began their approach into the cove. They bounded in, crashing powerfully through the waves, and up onto the beach. The horses stood and rested on the pebbles of the shore, their white ghost-like forms easily seen through the darkness.

Simon and Rebecca climbed down, still trembling slightly from the excitement, and looked around the cove. Through the grey night they could see a low cloud that hung across the hillside and shrouded the cliff above them. They could see the angular shapes of the rocks that had been sculpted by the breakers washing through their towering forms. The jagged cliffs created a wall that funnelled down to a river, which flowed through a flat flood plain. This was the mouth of Stowe Valley.

Along the top of the beach, where the cobbles of the shore met the soil of the land, the river had created a pool.

Simon stopped. "This must be the pool, but why aren't there any ducks?" he said thoughtfully.

Rebecca felt a shudder of cold sweep through her. "I don't like this place Simon, it has a creepy feel to it."

Simon felt a strange feeling too, as he looked into the waters of the pool. "Rebecca, do you remember what Nelleth said? That this place was dangerous.

Why do you suppose that would be?"

"I don't know. It was something about the sword's magic, but let's not stand here to find out." No sooner had she turned to walk on, a voice cackled through the darkness at the children. A voice that sounded gravelled, and ice cold.

"We are the witches of the ducking pool. What manner of human is this that carries the sword to our waters? This is the sleeping place of our magic. No other can thwart us here!"

From out of the cloud came hunched and twisted shapes that were so haggard and contorted that Rebecca barely conceived that they could be human. Some carried staffs, or were clothed in rags.

"We that were cast into the lake for our sorcerous ways are all powerful by night."

"What are they?" asked Rebecca.

"Now I know why this place is called Duckpool," said Simon. "It's a place where they used to put witches into the pool to see if they were a witch or not. If they sank and drowned then they were innocent, but if they floated they were guilty and burned. Either way they died."

"They're closing in on us!" cried Rebecca. "We're cut off from the valley."

* * * * * * *

On the cliff above Duckpool stood the lonely shape of a shadow man. He looked down through the mist and watched the two human forms edging back down the beach, their way ahead totally blocked. It was just as the Shadow Lord had foreseen.

* * * * * * *

Joe and the dragon had cunningly followed the Shadow Lord's armies as they swept across the land under the cover of night.

"They seem to have stopped," he said to Zilef. "I shall creep ahead alone. You are too big to follow me and the dark armies may see you from a distance. I need to know what they are doing."

So he and Zilef the dragon parted company upon the moor. He crept swiftly and silently forward under the cover of darkness. His light steps barely touched the ground. So gentle was his movement that hardly a blade of grass folded beneath him. He came to within two hundred metres of the group, and he crawled into a hollowed-out pit beneath a large rock. He was about to move forward again, when he saw that the armies had stopped moving across the way in front of him, and were moving towards the stone under which he lay.

He began to panic and for a moment he thought that he might have been discovered, but he could see no plausible reason how this was possible. He turned to retreat, but the shadow men had swirled around the back of the stone too. The figures didn't seem to come any closer, and Joe could see them clearly.

They seemed to be dancing and swirling round each other in some kind of trance. They beat their feet upon the ground and waved their arms fiendishly through the air around them. So wildly weird were their jerky movements that they looked more like puppets having their strings pulled by a phantom master.

Then through the middle of the spinning crowd, towering above them, was the creature Joe had been confronted by earlier that night. His bull's horns twitched as he threw aside the shadow people to clear a pathway. Behind him walked the hooded figure of the Shadow Lord. As he passed the crowd, they fell upon their knees and bowed their heads with every step.

The horned creature came right up to the very rock that Joe lay beneath. Then he also kneeled down.

Joe inched back as far as he could into the darkness out of fear that he would be discovered, but even kneeling, the creature was just tall enough to be incapable of seeing beneath the rock without further crouching down. The creature's head was obscured from Joe, but he was so close that he could see the silver sweat on its muscular chest that ran down to its abdomen, and the strange merging of human flesh with hair-covered skin where it became a horse's body. He felt flecks of moisture blow against his face, carried under the stone by the wind, from the monsters flared nostrils. He was terrifyingly close.

Then he saw the Shadow Lord's black robe trailing across the ground before him, as he rounded the very rock that Joe crouched beneath, and climbed up onto the top of it.

Joe was beside himself with fear, for he knew that his discovery could be just moments away.

Chapter Twelve

On The Rocks Of Land And Sea.

The sinister contorted forms encroached closer and closer towards Simon and Rebecca. They had retreated back onto the beach, but even the rocks of the cove seemed to be coming alive with movement.

As they edged their way along the cliff, they could hear hissing voices coming from within caves and hollows in the rock. Large purple eyes seemed to be glowing through the darkness within.

"If you just give us the sword", they growled, "then you will see the light of tomorrow, if not then in our Duckpool will be your sorrow!"

The voices chanted the same line, and for a second, it began to have a hypnotic effect, but Rebecca was not going to be taken so easily.

"I've had enough of this!" she said to Simon.

They had gone as far as they could along to the end of the cove. The low tide had pulled back from the rocky shore to the side of them, but there were movements from the rocks along the shore too.

Simon stepped forward to protect Rebecca from the ever-closing group.

"If we could just get down to the water," he said, "we should be able to get around the rocks to the next beach, Sandymouth."

Rebecca raised the sword, its gleam sparkled in her eyes, and before Simon knew what was going on she leapt forwards in front of him. As the first twisted, menacing creature came within reach of the blade, Rebecca decided to try to talk her way out of a fight first. "We don't mean any harm, just let us pass," she said positively.

The creature standing before her raised a large stick and swung for Rebecca. She blocked the stick with the sword and then swung back. Within an instant she was in the grips of battle once more.

Simon stood back in amazement at her sword skills, but then he noticed that when Rebecca was striking at the figures, for a second they would fall back, but then they rejoined the fight uninjured by the sword.

"Rebecca, it's not working," he cried out. "Nelleth said the sword's magic would be of no use here. We have to reach the water."

Rebecca turned her attack towards the beach, striking her way through with Simon crouched behind her. Occasionally she spun round to defend her back from the ghoulish figures until they reached a passage through the rocks.

"We can make it through here!" she cried, backing into the space whilst still fighting off her attackers. The two turned and ran through the gap with the fiendish shapes just behind them.

Under their feet lay the soft, wet sand from the tide. It dropped down into water-filled pools around the rocks, and at times, they were forced to wade in. One pool sloped to a very sudden depth, and they lunged forward and toppled to their necks in the cold seawater. Rebecca's armour seeped water through its joins around her shoulders, elbows and knees. It added extra weight to her escape when she finally reached high sand at the end of the pool. Still she raced on with Simon, with the water spilling out of every join in the armour.

Once they reached an open stretch of sand, their escape was further slowed as their feet sunk in almost to their ankles. It felt as if thousands of tiny hands were wrapping around them each time they touched the soft, wet grains, and they strained to pull free.

Occasional lightning lit the way but it was like a maze. They weaved through the jagged, angular rocks, darting through overhanging archways and through narrow passages of stone, but each time they rounded a new outcrop of rock, a gruesome figure lurked behind it in wait for them, but always Rebecca struck out wildly with the sword, or pushed them aside. Then as they rounded one such angular, rocky column, disaster struck and Simon was seized, caught within a witch's grip. He writhed and kicked to break free, but too strong were the long spidery hands that clasped his head and ran fumbling through his hair. "Rebecca, help!" he cried out.

Rebecca turned and walked determinedly back to the corner of rock where Simon's cries had come from, but all she heard were cackling voices and Simon's distant pleas. She was alone on the stretch of sand in amongst the shadowy rocks, with nothing more than the sound of the ocean.

* * * * * * *

On the open ground of the moors, Joe crouched beneath the rock that the Shadow Lord stood on. Thousands of shadow men were seated around it, and the monstrous whisperer that was neither man nor beast, was kneeling almost on top of him.

"My friends," the Shadow Lord's voice thundered out across the crowd, "I have brought you here to tell you of our plans and to share the news of our success with you."

A mighty cheer arose from the ground around the rock. When it had calmed a little, the Shadow Lord continued. "It seems there are not two humans that are against us but three."

A murmur went round the audience.

"The third, a child, has been spotted on the moor to the south by our most exalted of whisperers, our war maker. He was seen with another dragon!"

A cry of anguish arose from the crowd, and the Shadow Lord's voice cut the air with his own bitter anger.

"This third child is a boy. I want this boy found and brought before me, so that we may learn who he is, and how it can be that he rides with a dragon. Then, like the other two, he will know the real extent of my anger."

At this the crowd became a frenzy of cheering and movement. The figures again stamped upon the ground with their feet, with shouts and taunts of war.

Joe sat hardly daring to breathe beneath the stone. He was all the more scared that he was the object of hate that the crowd were so determined to smite.

The Shadow Lord spoke again. "At this very moment the humans have reached Duckpool with the sword. As I have foreseen, the sword's magic has caught the attention of the dark ones of Duckpool, who are pursuing them across the low tide-line to Sandymouth. There they will probably go by road to Stibb, and attempt to enter Stowe Wood from the top of the hill. We will divide our forces. Most of us will be within the trees at the edge of the wood, while some will wait in the hedgerow at the top of the field. When they are on the open ground half way down the field we will close in on them. I shall take the sword, and dispose of these treacherous humans myself. And tomorrow the world will be ours."

A mighty cheer came once more from the gathering that was so loud it hurt Joe's ears. Even so, Joe knew where the children were, and where the sword was, and furthermore he knew of the Shadow Lord's cunning plan to trap the children. But he had to work quickly because there wasn't much time.

The crowd moved away towards Stowe to set their trap, full of excitement and anticipation. Joe waited a moment until all seemed quiet, and he crept from his hiding place, and ran as fast as he could back to Zilef, before anyone could see.

But behind the cover of a set of rocks to his side, a pair of eyes watched his movements. Joe had been seen.

* * * * * * *

For over an hour Rebecca looked in amongst the rocks along the stretch of sand. There seemed to be little trace of the witches that had pursued them across the beach, only lots of trailing footprints that showed out as darker areas of churned up sand. Rebecca was very worried for her brother.

"Simon!" she would cry out, but there was no reply, and her voice was drowned out by the sound of the waves that were beginning to draw closer, as the tide moved in once more.

Still she searched the beach, until the water of the ebbing tide began to wash around her ankles. She paddled further, still calling out in the hope of a reply.

It was as she neared the last set of angular boulders before Sandymouth beach, that she heard a muffled sound in amongst a cluster of rocks that sat like a group of islands, out in the water. She listened again but heard nothing. Thinking that the sound might well have been a seagull she turned to walk on once more, when through the wind came a very distinctive cry.

"Help, somebody help!" the voice called out.

Rebecca waded into the water for she knew it to be her brother. She reached her knees when she heard the cry again and she rushed on. The water swirled around her waist and the waves washed against her in huge, white steps, while the depth continued to encroach. As she rounded the rock, the water was up to her chest.

There, spread out against the rock was Simon. He was tied tightly with his arms outstretched with twines of seaweed. It seemed to have grown around him, weaving and twisting itself about his limbs and chest so that he could hardly move. The water was up to his chin, and he coughed and spluttered. "Help Rebecca quickly, he cried out in panic, "we don't have much time and my feet are tied too!"

With that a wave washed over his head and he coughed again as he struggled for air.

Rebecca tugged at the seaweed. It was too strong and very slippery. Again she tried, but this time she slipped back into the water with a loud splash under the weight of the sword and her armour. Another wave washed over Simon's head. He had become completely covered and Simon could no longer breathe.

Chapter Thirteen

The Strangest Of Meetings.

As Joe and Zilef took off into the skies once more, the eyes of the Shadow Lord who had seen his escape were thoughtful. The boy that he had just seen reminded him so much of the one who had thrown the sword into the lake and disappeared. It couldn't be possible. Yet he looked the same.

"How could it be that this boy is alive now in my time?" he whispered to himself. "What magic is it? What mischievous ironic trick of destiny would bring this boy forward through the centuries? Well I shall not fail this time, and I will use irony and trickery to get that which is mine."

The Shadow Lord rejoined his army, and led them off in the direction of Stibb and Stowe Woods where they were to lie in wait

* * * * * * *

When Rebecca surfaced again she found that Simon was beneath the rising waters. She was quick to think and drew in a large breath. Then she went to Simon and blew her air into his mouth so that he could breathe it in.

Simon had desperately needed her air. His lungs
ached from wanting to breathe in, but he knew that
the cold water around him held only instant death.
There was a chaotic moment when he wasn't sure
what his sister was doing, but then when he felt the
flow of air coming into his mouth, he steadily
inhaled it from her lungs into his.

After several good breaths, she set to work on
releasing Simon's arms using the sword. She had to
be careful because it was extremely sharp and she
had to feel her way through the task. Every few
seconds she stopped to deliver more air to Simon
and then she continued to cut through the seaweed.

Once one arm was free, Simon was able to help by
pulling at some of the strands that bound him, and
finally both of them appeared at the surface of the
water together.

He was a little out of breath, and his first moments above the water were spent savouring deep lung-filled gasps of night air.

"Thank you Rebecca," he spluttered, "I really thought I would die, and I would have done without you."

Rebecca looked at him with a smile. She had always enjoyed being his little sister, but being bigger than him, and something of an object of admiration was something she was enjoying too. She was also very relieved to see that her brother was all right.

The two of them waded back into the shores of the beach, and together they paddled knee deep around the last set of rocks to Sandymouth.

At the top of the beach a giant waterfall tumbled over the cliff. Its white rumble of cascading water sparkled and twisted with the movements of the night wind. Great lines of rock strata zigzagged with the higher and lower reaches of the cliffs. The top of the beach was made up of pebbles, but down at the edge of the water, where the waves were pushing their way in, was a large open plain of sand. Only occasional rocks dotted the flat landscape until the end of the beach, marked by the long rectangular rocks that the two had jumped over on the sea horses.

It was a place that existed outside time, and for a

million years it had looked similar. The ocean had washed away at the rocks since the world had begun, claiming a little of the cliff each year, yet as the children stood there in the grey light of the night, it was as if they were the first people ever to look upon it, for it felt new. Their tracks were the first and last upon the sand as they made their way up the beach before the tide smoothed them over, concealing the secret of the night.

They walked up past the waterfall to the slope from the beach. There they found a track that took them to the top of the cliffs and onto a lane. Then they began a walk that was to be over a mile up the hill towards Stibb.

As they walked, Rebecca and Simon noticed thousands of tiny lantern-like lights in the hedgerow on either side of them.

"Do you suppose it's part of the magic from the sword?" Simon asked.

"It must be," said Rebecca, "Joe warned us that all sorts of things happen when the jewel is in the sword."

"He was certainly right about that!" Simon agreed. He thought back to his experience with the strange forms that had put him upon the rock at Duckpool. Then he added, "Let's hope that we don't have any more surprises tonight."

Rebecca's eyes fell upon the sword and the jewel

that sparkled at its centre. The two dragons on the blade shimmered brightly. She thought of her promise to Nelleth and she turned to Simon. "It isn't far now, we're almost back in Stibb. Then we can cross the field and go down into the woods to the lake. We've nearly made it."

They turned and strode on up the hill towards the lights of the village.

* * * * * * *

Joe and Zilef swooped low over the beach of Duckpool. They searched the rocks but the tide was in.

"Do you think they might have crossed the cliffs to Sandymouth?" asked Zilef.

"I'm not sure," came Joe's reply. "We shall do one more pass along the beaches, then we should check the cliff path and the road to the village. It will be light soon, we should find them then."

* * * * * * *

It was dawn when Simon and Rebecca reached the top of the hill. A dark orange light broke from the ridge on the opposite side of Stowe valley above the woods, casting strange, tall shadows upon the ground.

Both Simon and Rebecca were exhausted as they made their way along the road. The roofs and chimneys of the houses of Stibb village rose high into the dawn sky, and only the lonely form of a bird circled above them in the morning light.

"I can't believe we're nearly there", said Rebecca, as they passed through the small collection of houses.

They reached their own gateway and drive.

"I wish we could go in and sleep," said Simon. Then he noticed the open door. "Do you think Dad's okay?"

"I suppose we ought to take a quick look."

The two of them crept up the driveway and peered in through the window.

There, still asleep in the chair was their father, but Rebecca was still concerned. "I might just go in for a closer look," she said, "I really have to know that he's alright."

Simon was about to remind her that she was actually a grown up, and that if her father woke up, she would find herself in a very difficult situation, but she was already half way into the room through the open door.

She crept across the floor towards the familiar sleeping man. It was strange. He didn't look as big and strong through adult eyes. His hands that normally seemed so large compared to hers were not so large. She reached out to touch one that hung down at his side. It was warm, and she held it in hers, smiling upon his sleeping face.

But then he stirred and sighed in his sleep. Rebecca hardly dared to let go in case he should wake.

"Morning Princess," he murmured sleepily.

"Morning Dad," she whispered back.

She placed his hand upon the arm of his old chair, and crept silently back to the door. Once she was outside again she came across Simon.

"How is he?" he asked.

"He's fine, but I nearly blew it. I have to change back to me really soon."

The two made their way out onto the road and across to the lane that led down Iron Hill. In the distance the church tower and the houses of Kilkhampton were a silhouette in the brightening sky at the top of the valley. Below them were the trees of Stowe, which promised an end to their struggle. They were just a few minutes away from the lake, and then it would be over.

Half way down Iron Hill they turned along the muddy track that took them across to the field. As they reached the field and climbed the gate, around them everything was still, but they were not alone. In the middle of the ground stood the friendly outline of Joe.

At the sight of him their hearts soared and they raced across the wet morning grass towards him shouting and waving. "Joe we have the sword and jewel. We've got it!" they yelled out. "We've got it."

Their excited attention was so focussed upon Joe that they failed to notice the thousand or more shadow forms, emerging from the hedge behind them in an ever-decreasing circle. Joe stood motionless. He watched the children race ever nearer clutching the sword that could shift the balance of power between good and evil in an instant.

As they ran across the field, Simon glanced down at the sword. Something didn't look quite right with the jewel. They were within a few yards of Joe when Simon grabbed Rebecca by the arm and pulled her to a stop. "Rebecca, the light in the jewel on the sword, it's going dim! Why hasn't Joe run towards us? And why is he in the middle of this open field?"

Rebecca's blood became ice as she looked curiously at the light, which was down to a dim flicker inside the sword's jewel. Then she looked back to Simon. His worried eyes searched hers questioningly.

"This isn't right!" she gasped. "Something isn't right!"

She looked down at her beautiful armour. Its once bright shine was dull and smeared, and it began to disappear. Her curls of hair were retracting, and her hands began to shrink. The ground grew closer and closer, and Simon stammered, "Rebecca, look at you! You're changing!"

The sword became awkward and heavy in her hand, and she was a nine-year-old girl once more. The children looked around them and saw the thousands of angry faces of the shadow men as they came from every tree and hedge around the field. The trap was closing in by the minute upon their helpless victims.

"Joe!" Rebecca cried out. "What's happening?"

Then both of the children saw that Joe's form began to change before their eyes. His clothes became a long, dark cloak. His blonde hair became the cowl that concealed his face, as he stretched to his real height. The children cried out with despair. They had been deceived by his evil magic. For there before them, in his fullest gruesome glory, stood the Shadow Lord. His dreaded mocking laughter filled the dawn air. The sword was almost in his grasp, and he moved towards the tearful children.

Chapter Fourteen

The Final Push.

"No," cried Rebecca. "It's not fair!"

"Fair? What do you know of fairness?" laughed the Shadow Lord. "I have watched human kind for over a thousand years. Many times I have cast my dark form upon some place through the dreams of others. Wherever there was obsession with power, I was there. Whenever people caused fighting by blaming others for what they did not have, they carried my flag into battle. Whenever a country starved in the heat of drought while other countries sat by only watching, it was my shadow that kept the selfish away. My armies that you see before you, look at them, they are the selfish thoughts of human minds. They are not the evil of another world, but the evil of this one; shadows of all men who put themselves before others. If I carry the sword of truth, then all will believe in selfish thoughts such as these, and no-one will recognise my evil for what it is. For when evil becomes truth, all believe, and I become a god. Now give the sword of truth to me."

The figure held out his hand. His hypnotic power began to swirl around the children. They were powerless and they held out the sword.

A sudden down rush of air came from the sky above, and a great flapping noise sank upon the three figures. Zilef with Joe upon his back swooped, and in an instant, Zilef had thrust his weight upon the Shadow Lord's body. He stumbled back and released his grip upon the sword. Joe leapt from the dragon and picked it up. It sat in his hand as if it was a part of him, and its light sparkled brighter than ever.

The dragon Zilef stood before the Shadow Lord snarling with his claws raised. Next to him was Joe clutching the sword.

The Shadow Lord looked curiously at Joe, surprised by his boldness. "You are foolish to think that you are strong enough to beat me. Every day for over a thousand years I have thought of the moment when you cast the sword into the lake."

"And in all that time, I have thought of that moment too," replied Joe calmly.

The anger began to swell inside the Shadow Lord, and turning to his thousands of shadow men he cried out. "Attack!"

The crowd of figures that circled them rushed in, but their shadow weapons could not injure the dragon, and Joe was too swift. The thousands of shadow men vanished one by one into dust, with each flash of the blade and swipe of the dragon's claw, and within a few minutes, hardly any were left.

Then from the top of the field came a cry that filled the children with fear. Towards the group came the most terrifying of all the Shadow Lord's warriors. His bull's horns were directed at Joe as he charged in a full gallop across the open field. For a moment Zilef stepped forward, but raising an arm Joe said, "This is a battle that only the sword of truth can win. Step back Zilef."

He ran towards the figure with the sword raised, and at the last second he stepped aside, and thrust it with all his strength, deep into the creatures chest. A cry echoed across the valley, and the creature fell silent upon the ground. Then he too vanished into dust.

Zilef had destroyed the remaining shadow men and now he turned to the Shadow Lord. "You took Nelleth!" he cried angrily.

The Shadow Lord laughed mockingly and reached into the folds of his cloak, and drew his own black sword. He raised it into the air, and with an enraged cry, brought it down upon Zilef, but at the moment it was about to strike, the golden blade of the sword blocked it. At its handle stood Joe.

Again and again the Shadow Lord brought his sword upon the boy, and a shower of sparks rained from the black and gold metal as the swords met in mid flight, but each time, Joe blocked his blows. Then Joe fought back. The Shadow Lord was able to stop the attack from the sword, but it glanced powerfully from his own. He raised his own menacing sword once more, and the exchange of blows continued as the fight went on.

Slowly, they moved across the field and into the trees. Simon and Rebecca, and Zilef followed, anxious that Joe should not be injured, as the duel continued. The battle moved down the track and off in the direction of the lake, as Joe forced the Shadow Lord further from the world of men, and into the dense woodlands, which echoed with the clashing of gold and black.

Then Joe and the Shadow Lord passed under the gate and moved on towards the lake, until they were at the top of the bank exchanging blows. The Shadow Lord struggled to lift the sword now, weakened ever more by every strike of Joe's blade.

Finally, Joe brought his sword so swiftly against the Shadow Lord that he could not stop its shining incipience, as it struck through the black cloak, and into his opponent's side. He stumbled down the bank towards the water, clutching his wound as dust seeped from it into the air.

Joe stood on the top of the bank. The battle was won, and he found himself looking down curiously upon the figure. A look of relief flashed across his face, and from somewhere within his memory, he recalled being in the place where the Shadow Lord was standing at that moment, and now it was he that stood at the top of the bank, above the figure that once caused him to leap into the watery depths in fear of his life. And with a certain familiarity, Joe exclaimed, "You are beaten!"

The hooded figure struggled for breath still clutching his wound at his side. "Help me!" he groaned. "Please help me?"

Simon and Rebecca stood for a second as Joe put down his sword and moved down the bank, and then they followed.

"It's alright, I *will* help you," Joe said, and he leaned down to the crouched figure of the Shadow Lord.

But the Shadow Lord stood up straight and he held his black sword to Joe's chest laughing. "You're still as foolish as you are weak," he said mockingly. "Now, finally I will end this and kill you."

But he felt a small pair of hands grip him around his waist, and an almighty push sent him toppling off the bank. He splayed his arms out awkwardly to try to regain his balance, but he was already falling towards the water.

There was a brilliant flash, and a bang that echoed across the lake. The Shadow Lord was gone, sent back into the world of dreams by the magic of the lake and a sudden push.

In the place where he had stood, with her hands still raised from the push, was a nine-year-old girl. Her face wore a half-smile half-scowl expression, and she said, "maybe in another thousand years or so, but not today!"

"Rebecca you did it!" cried Simon.

"With a little help from Joe," she replied.

Joe raised the sword and cast it into the lake. "This time it stays there," he said, and Rebecca, Simon, Joe and the dragon stood upon the bank staring into the water, as the first of the new day's sunlight broke through the trees to light the ripples where the sword had landed, in the centre of the lake.

When Simon and Rebecca got home, they woke their father. They all looked extremely tired, and he suspected that his children and himself might be unwell, so they had the last day of the week off school to rest.

They were clearing away the table, when Rebecca's father came over to her. "I can't believe how quickly you're growing up," he said, as he watched her organising the dishes in the sink. Her and Simon began to laugh, and she turned around and replied, "Not me, tried it once and didn't like it!"

Her father shook his head, a little confused at what could possibly be so funny.

Joe himself returned to the woods. He had not only got back the sword, but he was also no longer lonely, for he had two friends who came to visit. He was missed at school on Monday morning. When the teacher, Miss Jones, asked Rebecca and Simon where he was, they said he had left the school, which was true. They sat and thought of Joe out somewhere in the woods while they did the register.

"And now for our work," Miss Jones announced. "As part of our story writing I thought we should learn a little about legends. Does anyone know anything about our own local legend, the one about the boy with the golden sword who lives within Stowe Woods?".........

The story of the Sword Watchers and the secret legend of Stowe Wood has now been told, and that is the end of the saga. Well, almost. When the children were collected from school their father sat deep in thought in the old blue Landrover. "I don't suppose you two know where that old sword is?" he asked.

A half-scowl, half-smile spread across Rebecca's face, and the answer they gave..... is another story.

The End